Sophie's Little Angel
Juliet Harmer

COLLINS

First published William Collins Sons & Co Ltd 1987
© Text and illustrations Juliet Harmer 1987
Printed in Hong Kong by Wing King Tong Co. Ltd.

When Sophie was six years old, she went to live in the country. Inside, everything felt just the same as it had in her old house, but outside, everything was quite different.

First Sophie explored the garden. What a lot there was to discover! She took her teddy to show him all the new and exciting things.

There was a swing under a cherry tree, and there were some steps leading to a little pool of water lilies. There were flowers everywhere, and birds singing, and butterflies in the air. And how sweet everything smelt!

But best of all, there was a big tree, with a ladder that went up to a little wooden tree house. At the very end of the garden, there was a gate. And through the gate, a grassy path led into an orchard, where long grass grew under the old trees.

Sophie sat down under a tree filled with blossom.
Suddenly, she saw something lying in the
grass. She picked it up, and held it in her hand.

It was a tiny, wooden angel. Very carefully, she put it in her pocket, tucked her teddy under her arm, and went back to the cottage.

Sophie wanted to put the little angel in a special place beside her bed. In the wall there was a tiny hole, and the angel fitted perfectly. "You can live there," said Sophie, "you can bring me good dreams at night."

The next morning, Sophie woke up early, and ran into the garden. There was still dew on the grass, and a little squirrel sat perfectly still on the wall by the gate to the orchard.

"The orchard is a magic place," thought Sophie. "I know, I shall make a little garden there and when it is ready, I shall bring the angel to show it to her, and we shall have a celebration."

So the next Saturday, Sophie spent her birthday money on five packets of seeds, and a little gardening set. She found a sunny patch and carefully cleared away the weeds. Then she collected a basket of shells and pebbles and circled the garden to make it pretty. Next, she scattered the seeds, carefully covered them up, and gave them a good drink.

Every morning, Sophie went to look at her seeds. Eventually, tiny green shoots began to push through the earth. Soon there were little buds on top of the stalks and finally, one morning, a crumpled poppy opened its bright red petals to the sun.

Cornflowers, poppies, marigolds, nasturtiums and sunflowers soon filled the little garden. And when they were all out Sophie knew it was midsummer and time for the angel's picnic. So she gathered up her teddies, put the angel in her pocket, filled her basket with tea things and went into the orchard.

Sophie spread a tablecloth on the green grass beside the little garden and arranged the food. When everything was ready she felt in her pocket. It was time for the angel to see the beautiful garden. Very carefully, she settled her in the place of honour. The picnic was perfect.

When it was all over, Sophie put the tea things
back in the basket, and shook out the tablecloth
so that the birds could have the crumbs.
"We must go home now, little angel," she said.
"It will be dark soon."

The summer slipped into autumn and the leaves on the trees turned to gold. Michaelmas daisies filled the garden, and in the orchard there were blackberries and plums and rosy apples. Soon it was too dark to play in the garden after tea. There were witches on television, and talk of Christmas. Sometimes a fox barked in the darkness, and on frosty nights, the stars were· very bright. Wherever she went, Sophie kept her little angel close by.

One morning, Sophie looked out of her window, and found that everything she saw, everywhere she looked, was quite white. She thought of the birds and how hungry they would be if they could not find their food. So she put on her coat and boots and went out into the garden.
"Here you are," she called softly to the birds.
And she scattered crumbs for them to eat.

The very next night was Christmas Eve. Sophie hung up her stocking, said a special goodnight to her angel, closed her eyes, and heard the church bells across the snowy fields.

What excitement to wake up in the morning and see her stocking filled with presents. Was it time to go into the big bed? Sophie drew back the curtains to see how light it was. She looked across the garden to the orchard. "Oh!" She held her breath. For there, in the orchard, was the most beautiful Christmas tree she had ever seen. All the animals of the forest had gathered round it, and there, on the very top, was her tiny wooden angel.

This book is dedicated to
Bill and Jessie and Lola
(and to my cat Sam)

British Library Cataloguing in Publication Data

Harmer, Juliet
   Sophie's little angel.
   I. Title
   823'.914[J]   PZ7

   ISBN 0-00-191123-6